# THE GHOST IN THE ARTROOM

**Roger Stevens**

*Illustrated by* Bob Doucet

# Titles in First Flight

Badger Publishing Limited
15 Wedgwood Gate, Pin Green Industrial Estate,
Stevenage, Hertfordshire SG1 4SU
Telephone: 01438 356907. Fax: 01438 747015
www.badger-publishing.co.uk
enquiries@badger-publishing.co.uk

The Ghost in the Artroom ISBN 1 84424 843 7

Text © Roger Stevens 2006
Complete work © Badger Publishing Limited 2006

Series Editor: Jonny Zucker
Publisher: David Jamieson
Commissioning Editor: Carrie Lewis
Editor: Paul Martin
Design: Fiona Grant
Illustration: Bob Doucet
Printed and bound in China through Colorcraft Ltd., Hong Kong

# THE GHOST IN THE ARTROOM

**Roger Stevens**

It was a Wednesday,
Five o'clock.
October, getting dark.
The Artroom
Quiet as quiet.
The wind – singing on the playground
A sad song.
But that was all.
The Artroom
Quiet as quiet.

The class had been painting.
Big blue blobs of sky,
Mucky green fields,
A stick man and a stick dog.

I was tired.
I heard a dog barking.
A dog barking outside
On the playground.
Was it hurt?

It was a hurt kind of a bark.
A sob, more than a bark.
The dog was so sad.

I put down the painting
And went outside
To take a look.
Teachers don't like dogs on the playground.
They make a mess.
They poo.
It's bad.

It was dark outside.
It was cold.
I looked around.
There was no dog.
Only dark shadows
And the wind singing
A sad song.

One week later,
Wednesday, five o'clock
Alone in the Artroom
I heard it again.
The dog on the playground
Barking at the moon.
I don't know why
But it made me shiver.

I went outside to look.
There was the moon.
The night sky full of stars.
The old Victorian school
Looked dark and creepy
But there was no dog.

I could still hear it.
A sad sound.
It was coming from my store room
Where I stored my paper and paints,
My pencils and brushes.

I crept across the room
And listened at the door.
There was no mistake.
There was the sound.
Now it was a soft growl.
As if the dog was just there
Behind the door.

I opened the door.
Slowly, now.
Slowly.
The door creaked.
Easy now.

There was no dog.
No scary dog
Or angry dog
Or even a friendly dog.
The store room was empty.

But I could still hear the low growl.
The sound of a sad dog.
Or hurt.
Or lost.

That was it.
It was the sound of a lost dog.
I looked around.
There was nothing there.
I looked up.
There was a trapdoor in the ceiling
Of my store room
But I'd never opened it.

I listened to the lost dog.
It was up there
In the school loft.
And I heard another sound.
A tip-tapping sound.
Tip-tap.
Tip-tap.
The sound of wood upon wood
Or bone upon bone.

It was very creepy.
Okay, I admit it,
I was a little bit scared.
So I did
What any teacher would do.
I went home.

Over the next few months,
As Autumn gave way to Christmas,
And Christmas to the cold winds of
The new year,
I often heard the sounds.
Never when the room was full
Of the warm talk
Of students working
Or the warm smell of fresh paint
on paper.

But when the room was quiet
And I was on my own,
Only then I'd hear the soft bark
And the tip-tapping
Tip-tap
Tip-tap
Tip-tap
Of the lost dog.

And then
Everywhere began to turn green
And January and February were over
And it was Easter.

It was all changing.
A new life for the school,
A new life for me.
The school was moving to a new place
down the road.
Leaving the tiny classrooms,
The stinky toilets and creaky desks
And I was leaving too.

Saying goodbye to the teachers,
My friends, and the students
And the Artroom.

And so it was
That on the last day of term,
Ken, the caretaker, and I
Carried the ladder
Through the sad, empty classroom
And into the store room.
Ken pushed the ladder up to the trapdoor,
And slowly went up.
He looked down at me.
I nodded.
He took a deep breath
And banged the trapdoor open.

Muck and dust
Filled the small space.
Ken sneezed.
But in my mind I could only hear
The soft doggy sounds,
The tip-tap
Tip-tap.

Darkness spilled out.
Ken crawled into the hole,
with his torch.
I heard him gasp.

Soon we both stood in the loft,
And looked down at what we could see
Hardly believing our eyes.
Lying between the beams,
Curled in the dust of a century,
Dull – white in the torch light
The skeleton of a dog,

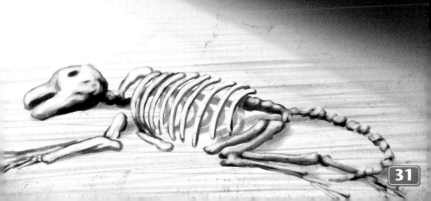

And in its jaws
Clenched forever
A stick.

(I did indeed leave the school.
The dog's skeleton was cleaned and
is now an exhibit in the school's new
science laboratory).

GHOST DOG

Leabharlanna Fhine Gall